Monster Mountain

Thunderbelle's Song

Karen Wallace

Illustrated by
Guy Parker-Rees

ORCHARD BOOKS

RENEWALS 0161 253 7180

1 3 FEB 2012   1 3 OCT 2012

2 3 APR 2013

1 0 MAY 2012

1 5 AUG 2013

2 4 MAY 2012

2 5 MAR 2014

1 6 AUG 2012   − 4 DEC 2015

2 8 AUG 2012

RADCLIFFE 1 8 MAR 2011

1 9 APR 2011

−6 MAY 2011

Please return/renew this item
by the last date shown.
Books may also be renewed by
phone or the Internet. 1 2 SEP 2011

1 5 DEC 2011

www.bury.gov.uk/libraries

For Penny Morris
K.W.
For Alex and Alfie,
with love
G. P-R.

First published in 2007 by Orchard Books
First paperback publication in 2008

ORCHARD BOOKS
338 Euston Road, London NW1 3BH
Orchard Books Australia
Level 17/207 Kent St, Sydney, NSW 2000

ISBN 978 1 84362 620 6 (hardback)
ISBN 978 1 84362 628 2 (paperback)

1 3 5 7 9 10 8 6 4 2 (hardback)
1 3 5 7 9 10 8 6 4 2 (paperback)

Printed in China

Orchard Books is a division of Hachette Children's Books,
an Hachette Livre UK company.

www.orchardbooks.co.uk

Thunderbelle lay in bed listening.
A bird chirped, a frog croaked and
a woodpecker tapped a tree.
It was like lovely music.

Thunderbelle jumped out of
bed and ran to the Brilliant
Ideas gong.
She banged it as loudly as she
could. **Bong! Bong! Bong!**

The other monsters came quickly.
Clodbuster landed
in a parachute.

Roxorus roared up
on his skateboard.

Mudmighty rolled
down the mountain
like a ball.

Pipsquawk fluttered onto her favourite branch. "What's your brilliant idea?"

Thunderbelle grinned. "Let's make our own music on Monster Mountain!"

Everyone clapped and cheered.
There was only one problem. No
one knew how to play anything.

Pipsquawk thought hard. She had her best ideas upside down.

"Let's make our own instruments and play them!"

"Pipsquawk! You're a genius!" cried
Thunderbelle.
The monsters ran off to find
something to play.

Roxorus curled a piece of bark into a ring. Then he stretched a leaf over the top.

When he hit the leaf with a stick,
it sounded like the best drum in
the world!

Mudmighty looked at the rows
and rows of carrots and onions in
his garden.
There was nothing that would
make a good sound.

Then he remembered the jar of
dried peas in his cupboard. "Yes!"
he thought. "I've got the best
rattle ever!"

Pipsquawk found a bent branch in
the forest. It was the perfect shape
for a harp.

She found thin strong vines for the strings and played the harp with her feet. It sounded fantastic!

Clodbuster was having
fun. First he made
a guitar.

Then he made
a piano.

Then he made a hooter. He tried them all but he liked the hooter best.
It made the loudest noise.

Thunderbelle couldn't find anything
to play.
She tried hitting a saucepan with
a spoon.

She tried bashing a lid with a fork.
But it was no good. Everything
sounded terrible.

"What am I going to do?" cried
Thunderbelle.

"I know! I'll dress myself up! That
always helps!"

Thunderbelle pulled on her frilliest pink dress. She put on her biggest pink hat.

She squeezed into her sparkliest
pink shoes.
Then she twirled around her room
and thought very very hard.

Thunderbelle remembered how the
birds chirped and the frogs croaked.
"I shall sing," she cried. "I don't
have to play anything!"

At teatime, the monsters met in the
meadow. "Where's Thunderbelle?"
asked Roxorus. "She's late."

Just then, Thunderbelle ran into the meadow.

She bowed. Then she stood with her arms apart.

Pipsquawk understood
immediately.
"Ready! Steady! Go!"
she squawked.

Clodbuster blew a terrific
TOOT on his hooter.

Mudmighty rattled
his huge jar
of peas.

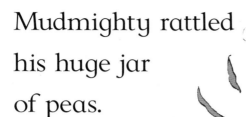

Roxorus banged
his drum.

Pipsquawk ran
up and down on
her harp strings.

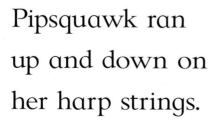

Thunderbelle took a deep breath and began to sing I LOVE MONSTER MOUNTAIN. It was everyone's favourite song.